Play On!

Story by Carmel Reilly

Illustrations by Martin Fagan

NELSON
CENGAGE Learning

Play On!

Text: Carmel Reilly
Series consultant: Annette Smith
Publishing editor: Simone Calderwood
Editor: Annabel Smith
Designer: Karen Mayo
Series designers: James Lowe and
   Karen Mayo
Illustrations: Martin Fagan
Production controller: Erin Dowling

PM Guided Reading
Ruby Level 28

Gadget Girl
Special Effects: Bringing Movies to Life
Banding Together
Play On!
The Power of Wind
Time and Clocks
Amazing Stories of Survival
Wildfire
Southern Skies
Shipwrecked!

Text © 2016 Cengage Learning Australia Pty Limited
Illustrations © 2016 Cengage Learning Australia Pty Limited

ISBN 978 0 17 0373081

Cengage Learning Australia
Level 7, 80 Dorcas Street
South Melbourne, Victoria Australia 3205
Phone: 1300 790 853

Cengage Learning New Zealand
Unit 4B Rosedale Office Park
331 Rosedale Road, Albany, North Shore NZ 0632
Phone: 0800 449 725

For learning solutions, visit **cengage.com.au**

Printed in China by 1010 Printing International Ltd
1 2 3 4 5 6 7 20 19 18 17 16

CONTENTS

CHAPTER 1
On the Way

Sam

Sam was late for basketball practice. He was running towards the gym when, out of the corner of his eye, he glimpsed a bright red, yellow and blue poster outside the school hall. He hastily changed direction so he could read it.

WANTED

Actors, singers, dancers, artists, stage hands, assistant directors. We need you for our all-school play,

THE GREAT WALDO

A musical adventure set in a circus.

Roll up, roll up for auditions!
When: This Thursday, 1pm
Where: The school hall

For more information, see Ms Norton (Drama teacher)

The Great Waldo! Sam could hardly believe it.
They were his favourite stories. He had read the
books at least ten times when he was younger.
Now there was a play as well. He thought about
all the different characters in the stories. The main
character was Waldo, the mischievous circus clown
who performed tricks, told hilarious jokes and –
most importantly – solved mysteries, such as the
mystery of the missing elephant.

Then there were other characters, such as Horace
the lion tamer, Archie and Chloe the acrobats,
Clem the odd-job man and Martha the circus
manager. And finally, there was Ronaldo the devious
ringmaster, who was always trying to outsmart
Waldo. Somehow, though, Waldo always managed
to succeed and made Ronaldo look extremely silly.

Sam laughed to himself as he recalled some of the antics of his favourite book characters. He was still smiling when he burst through the doors of the gym.

"Is something amusing, Sam?" asked Mr Gilmore, the basketball coach.

Sam shook his head, and his smile faded. "Sorry I'm late," he said.

Mr Gilmore scowled. "You know the rules, Sam. It is important that everyone is punctual and ready for basketball practice. And you know we need to work extremely hard if we are going to make it to the finals."

"Late again," said his friend Zane, elbowing Sam playfully. "Anyone would think you didn't want to be here!"

Sam didn't have time to reply. A basketball was soaring through the air towards him and he had to leap high to catch it. Sam knew that he was a skilful player, but that he needed to improve. The truth was that although he enjoyed playing basketball, he didn't feel the same passion and drive that other players did about basketball. His father and grandfather had been basketball champions when they were young, and his mother represented the state at hockey. Everyone in his family loved sport.

Recently, though, Sam had been having doubts. Perhaps he wasn't really that interested in basketball any more. And, he had been thinking about other things, such as acting. His dad was convinced that Sam was going to be a sports champion like him. He was always telling Sam not to be distracted and to practise more. But it was such a coincidence seeing the poster for the play today. Sam loved the idea of being on stage and transforming himself into another character for an hour or two. If he could be part of the school play, it wouldn't really affect basketball practice.

Maybe ... he thought, *maybe this is my opportunity.*

CHAPTER 2
Who Do You Really Want to Be?

 Miles

Miles smiled. This was his first drama class with Ms Norton and he had loved every minute of it. Ms Norton was so enthusiastic!

"That was fantastic, everyone!" said Ms Norton, smiling brightly. "You've been a wonderful group of students."

When the class ended, Ms Norton called Miles over.

"Miles," she said, "are you considering auditioning for a part in *The Great Waldo* play?"

"Yes, I am," Miles replied.

"Excellent," Ms Norton said. "And which role will you try out for?"

Miles felt slightly nervous. He didn't want to seem overly confident. "I would love to play the main role of Waldo," he said. "Or Ronaldo. I imagine that Ronaldo could be an interesting character to play, too."

Ms Norton laughed. "They are wonderful characters, aren't they? If you like, you can audition for both parts."

"Really? I would love to," said Miles. Then he added, "Which book is the play based on?"

"The first book, but a few changes have been inserted."

"*The Mystery of the Missing Elephant* is my favourite book!" said Miles, enthusiastically.

"So, tell me, how would you feel if you got the part of the elephant?" asked Ms Norton, with a twinkle in her eye.

11

Miles was surprised. He thought for a moment, then said, "Well, I would love to get a big role, and the elephant is very big!"

Ms Norton laughed.

"But, seriously, if I wasn't successful in getting a main role, that would be fine," said Miles. "I know that everyone's part in a play is important, no matter what it is."

"You have been on stage before, haven't you?" asked Ms Norton.

"Yes, I have been in a few performances with my drama group," Miles said. "And I can sing and dance, too," he added.

"I thought so. I could tell that you have some acting experience," said Ms Norton. "As you know, this play also includes a few singing and dancing routines, so it sounds like it could be just your cup of tea."

Miles grinned. "I would really love to be a part of the play. We've never performed a proper play at school like this before. It's very exciting."

"I'm glad you think so," said Ms Norton. "So, I'll see you on Thursday, then?"

"Yes, you will," Miles said, as he headed for the door, already thinking about how he could prepare for the audition.

Miles didn't often feel nervous when taking part in auditions, but, a few days later, when he stood on the stage in the school hall in front of Ms Norton and Mr Phipps, the principal, his knees began to tremble. There were other people watching, too. Some of the students who were also auditioning were waiting in the wings. He moved forward and read some lines from the script in his hand, but his voice sounded wooden and forced.

Ms Norton looked at him from across the table where she sat with Mr Phipps.

"Miles, why don't you begin again and take some deep breaths to relax," she said. "Try not to think about us."

Miles inhaled deeply and focused on a point at the back of the hall. There was a small painting he hadn't noticed before. He imagined it was a face in the crowd at the circus, looking at him and encouraging him. Gradually, he began to relax and the words from the script flew out of his mouth like birds freed from a cage. His body became supple and rubbery, like a clown's body, and his walk became loose and springy. He extended his mouth into a silly grin and opened his eyes wide.

"Miles has become Waldo!" he heard someone behind him whisper, as he bounded towards the front of the stage.

When he had finished his piece, Miles performed a short song, to demonstrate to Ms Norton and Mr Phipps that he could sing, as well.

"Excellent performance," said Mr Phipps, making a note on the pad in front of him.

"Yes, most enjoyable," said Ms Norton, nodding in agreement.

"Thank you," Miles said.

In the wings next to him, he caught sight of his friends Jemima and Aliya, grinning and giving him the thumbs up.

As he walked off the stage, he bumped into the boy who was next in line. "Oh, sorry," he said.

Miles recognised the boy as Sam, one of the school's star basketball players, and one of the most popular kids at school. They were in a different class and didn't really know each other, so he was surprised when Sam spoke to him.

"You were amazing," Sam said.

"Really?" said Miles. "Thanks. Good luck with your audition."

"I'll need it!" Sam laughed. "Do you have any tips?"

Miles laughed, too. "Not really – just try to relax."

Sam grinned. "Thanks!"

CHAPTER 3
New Friendships

 Sam

Sam walked home from school, bouncing his basketball and lost in thought. He could hardly believe what had happened. The list of roles for the play had been posted on the bulletin board just before the end of the school day. He had run straight from his class to find he had landed a part! He was going to be the lion tamer's assistant. It was a small role, but he did have a few lines. The boy, Miles, who he had spoken to at the audition, had won the role of Waldo, which was no surprise. Miles was a gifted actor.

When Sam got home, his mum and dad were in the kitchen, deep in conversation. He was about to tell them his good news when Dad turned to him with a worried expression on his face.

"I have been talking to Mr Gilmore, Sam. He says you are not taking your basketball practice seriously enough." Dad shook his head with disappointment.

"You realise you can make a huge difference in the team, don't you? It could ultimately be you who determines if the team is placed in the finals or not."

Sam felt a tense knot in his stomach. He couldn't let his dad, or the team, down. "I'm sorry. I promise I'll work harder."

He thought about the play. It certainly wasn't the right time to tell his parents about it. Once he had improved at basketball, he could share his news. Besides, he only had a small role in the play, so it wouldn't take much time away from practice. Sam was confident that he could still focus on basketball and not let anyone down.

A few weeks later, Sam stood in the centre of the
hall, facing the stage. All the characters in the play
were together for an after-school dress rehearsal.
Sam watched Miles performing as Waldo and
Jemima performing as Ronaldo. Finally, after a few
rehearsals, he was beginning to understand what
the play was going to be like when it was ready
to be performed. He held the script and read it,
while Miles and Jemima practised their lines and
rehearsed their movements. Sam prompted them
if they forgot something.

"What is that?!" screamed Ronaldo, pointing at
a mop and bucket.

"That is my secret weapon," said Waldo, leaning
forward and waving the mop.

Sam laughed. He had seen this performance
several times, and each time it made him laugh
out loud. They were hilarious.

Sam was thoroughly enjoying the rehearsals. He had achieved so much – more than he could ever have imagined. In the last three weeks, he had learnt eight songs, knew his own lines and (because he had been prompting Miles and Jemima) most of Waldo and Ronaldo's lines, as well. He had also helped Mr Potter, the school caretaker, to make and paint some of the props for the play, and he had entertained the younger cast members by teaching them basketball tricks. But, the most valuable thing of all was that he had established close friendships with Miles, Jemima and Aliya, people he had never really spent time with before.

The last few weeks had been so hectic. He rushed between school, play rehearsals and basketball practice, yet he had never felt so happy and satisfied, apart from the small, niggling worries that he kept placing to the back of his mind. So far, his basketball practice and rehearsals hadn't clashed, but he knew that in the next weeks, there were going to be more rehearsals for the play, and he would have to miss some to attend basketball practice.

And, he still hadn't told his parents about his new activity.

CHAPTER 4

A Big Break

 Miles

Miles leapt from one foot to the other. "Look at me!" he cried.

Suddenly, he froze. "Oh! I can't remember the next line." He glanced towards Sam, who was standing in the middle of the hall, watching Miles and the other performers rehearse their lines.

"I'm going to dive into this bucket," prompted Sam, without referring to the script in his hand. "That's your next line."

Miles shook his head. "I can't believe I forgot that!" he muttered.

"Well, you definitely have a lot of lines to learn," said Sam.

Miles laughed. "Yes, but you've managed to memorise most of them, and you know Jemima's lines as well!"

"That's because I hear them all the time. Besides, there's no pressure for me to learn them. I don't have to feel nervous about getting things wrong."

Ms Norton clapped her hands. "Miles and Jemima, let's start this scene again from the beginning."

"All right," Miles said, picking up his bucket and mop and carrying them to the back of the stage.

"Everyone, please move into your positions," added Ms Norton, directing people to various places on the stage.

The ringmaster, lion tamer and everyone who was going to be in the crowd gathered around the edges of the make-believe circus ring.

Miles moved quickly from the back of the stage to the front. He gestured widely with his arms and held them open.

"I am the Great Waldo, the extraordinary clown!" he exclaimed. "And I'm here to entertain you!"

After rehearsals, Miles walked across the playground with Sam. They were talking excitedly about a new TV program.

"That show is brilliant. I would love to be in it," said Miles.

"You should audition for it," said Sam, enthusiastically.

Just then, Sam's friend, Zane, jogged by, bouncing a basketball.

"Hey!" he called. "Do you want to shoot a few hoops before we go back to class?"

There was a basketball ring at the end of a building, not far from where they were walking.

"Sure!" replied Sam. "Come on, Miles."

Zane threw the ball to Sam who leapt up, bounced the ball a few steps and then slammed it into the ring. He caught it as it fell back towards him, then he threw it to Miles who bounced it once, slowed to aim and thrust the ball high into the air.

"Hey, I didn't know about your hidden talent!" said Sam, as the ball hit the rim of the ring and toppled inside.

"Neither did I," said Miles, laughing and stepping forward to scoop up the ball.

Just then, Zane whizzed past to catch the ball, too.

He hadn't realised that Miles was going to pick it up, and when he did, he was too late to stop. Miles was just bending down as Zane hurtled towards him, knocking him sideways. There was a loud thump and a cry of pain as Miles fell awkwardly to the ground.

"I'm really sorry!" cried Zane, bending down to help Miles up. "Are you injured?"

For a moment, Miles didn't move. All he could feel was a searing pain in his leg. He felt his lip quiver as he tried to say something.

"What is it?" said Sam, anxiously.

"My leg," whispered Miles. "There's something wrong with my leg."

Miles felt so miserable. An ambulance had taken him from school and whisked him to the nearest hospital. His mum had rushed from work and met him in the emergency ward. An X-ray confirmed that his leg was broken. By the time he got home, it was late in the evening and his lower leg was covered in plaster and enclosed in a moon boot.

Miles didn't sleep well that night. It wasn't just the pain or the fact that he couldn't move around in bed. His real problem was that it was obvious he wouldn't be able to perform as Waldo. He couldn't leap about like Waldo. He couldn't run from the lion or chase Ronaldo. Not unless he did it in a wheelchair! He knew, realistically, that his dream of being the lead character in the school play was over. The pain of missing out on performing was far more painful than his broken leg.

CHAPTER 5
Time to Choose

 Sam

For the very first time, Sam didn't enjoy rehearsals. The hall was unusually quiet without Miles, or, perhaps more accurately, without Miles playing the part of Waldo. For two days, the cast spent lunchtime rehearsing their songs and routines. Then, on the third day, Miles appeared. He hobbled awkwardly into the hall on crutches. As he came towards the stage, everyone started to clap, and Miles looked around the hall in surprise.

"Welcome back, Miles!" said Ms Norton. "Sam, could you get a chair for Miles, please?" she added.

Sam dragged a chair over to where they were all gathered. Everyone else sat down on the floor, and Miles, who was towering over the others, said, "I am the king!"

"That's just what Waldo would say," said Jemima, laughing.

"Not this Waldo," said Miles, making a miserable face.

Ms Norton smiled and spoke. "As you are all aware, Miles will unfortunately not be able to continue in his role as Waldo. So I have decided to re-shuffle some of the actors and roles. Jemima, we think you would make an excellent Waldo in Miles's absence."

The group applauded. Jemima was a good choice because she had a good voice. Waldo did a lot of singing.

Ms Norton continued. "We have decided to give Jemima's old role to Sam."

Sam looked up, startled. He hadn't expected to change his role. A small explosion of excitement ran through him.

"Sam, you have memorised all of the lines," said Ms Norton. "All you need to do is to learn Ronaldo's solo and practise a few dance routines."

Sam glanced up at Miles, who nodded to him and grinned. Sam smiled back, but he felt slightly ill, as though he was taking away Miles's opportunity of becoming a star. "What about Miles?" Sam blurted out. "Is there a role for him?"

"Actually, there is!" said Ms Norton, smiling. "Miles is going to have a new role, which is really your old role, Sam, but we have included several new lines. Miles is also going to sing some breakout solos in the chorus songs. He will still be on the stage, but he won't have to move around too much."

When the meeting was over, Sam picked up Miles's crutches and helped him to his feet.

"My bad break has become a good break for you," said Miles, laughing.

"I'm really sorry," said Sam.

"Don't be. To be honest, I was extremely disappointed at first, but I'm pleased with Ms Norton's new arrangement. Even though I won't play the character of Waldo, I'll still have the opportunity to sing and be on stage."

Sam nodded.

"But you should be looking happier. You are now playing Ronaldo. That will be incredible!" said Miles.

Sam felt a knot in the pit of his stomach. "I would

feel better if all these extra rehearsals didn't clash with basketball practice. And if my parents were happy about me being in the play."

Miles frowned. "Don't they like it?"

"They still don't know," said Sam, glumly.

It was dinner time, and Sam and his parents had almost finished eating dessert. Sam had waited until the end of dinner to explain to his parents about the play. He had waited until everyone was relaxed and no longer discussing basketball. After he told them, Sam's dad was suddenly very quiet, which was unusual as he was one of the most talkative people Sam knew. But now, just for a few seconds, Sam realised that his dad didn't quite know what to say. He was lost for words.

"Sam, that is amazing news!" said Mum.
"I didn't know you were interested in acting.
And to get such a major part is fantastic. I'm very
proud of you."

Sam waited for his father to add something.

"I suppose you are going to have a number of
rehearsals after school," he said at last.

"I might not be able to attend all the basketball
practice sessions," said Sam, thinking that he should
mention that fact. "But, I've been practising really
hard, and the team has been performing well.
And it's only for the next few weeks."

"That's true," said Dad, thoughtfully. "But you
will have the semi-finals in the next few weeks,
too, and this is a crucial time. You are a key player."

Sam thought for a moment. "But some of the
other players have really improved. Like Zane.
He's terrific."

"Hmm," said Dad, sounding unconvinced.
"It wouldn't hurt if you miss a play rehearsal or two,
would it?"

"We only have limited time to rehearse before
the play goes on, and I can't let everyone down,"
said Sam. He looked at Dad, willing him to see
his point of view.

"Well, the same applies to the basketball team. Perhaps you should have thought of that before you auditioned for this play," said Dad, sternly. "You can't let your team down. You've been playing basketball for five years, but you've only been in this play a few weeks."

"Don't worry, Dad," said Sam. "I'll make sure I can do both. And if I miss a basketball practice session, then I will work twice as hard at the next one."

CHAPTER 6
Not Just a Stage

 Miles

Miles was surprised at how skilful he was at using his crutches. It wasn't long before he could move almost as quickly as he could normally, although of course he couldn't run, dance or do anything gymnastic. In the first few days back at school, Ms Norton had also asked him to help her with some extra work. She had decided that, as there were more rehearsals, she needed an assistant director.

"Actually, it was Sam's suggestion," she said. "He mentioned that players sometimes assist the coach in his basketball team."

At first, Miles wasn't convinced that he wanted to be an assistant director. But soon, he realised that he really liked it and that he was good at it. He had more acting experience than most of the other students in the play. He loved advising them and giving suggestions about performances.

"Thanks," Miles said to Sam a few days later. "It's been surprisingly good helping Ms Norton."

Sam smiled. "I thought you would like it."

"How's your basketball?" Miles asked.

"The team has been playing really well. We've won our last four games. If we win this next one, we'll get into the semi-finals. If we win games in the semi-finals round, the final will be on the same day as the opening of the play."

"Oh, no," said Miles.

"It's a challenge. There are so many practice drills, and getting up early on Saturday mornings for the games is really difficult after such long weeks. Dad says I'm the best in the team and they need me. But I actually think there are lots of valuable players in the team now, as we've all had to work together. Dad doesn't realise this, because for some ridiculous reason he thinks I'm the best."

"So being in a basketball team and being in a play is the same thing really, isn't it?" said Miles, thoughtfully. "We all work together to make something amazing. Then, something happens, like when I broke my leg, and we have to make adjustments. The play still goes on, just a little differently."

"Maybe the play won't be quite as good without you as Waldo and Jemima as Ronaldo?" said Sam.

"Maybe," said Miles. "Or maybe it will be better! It doesn't matter, because between us all, it's going to be brilliant, no matter what!"

CHAPTER 7
Teamwork

 Sam

Ms Norton had organised a music and drama night as a preview to *The Great Waldo* play that would be shown a week later. There would be all kinds of performances, including a short scene from the play, performed by Sam, Jemima and Miles.

Sam peeked out from behind the curtains. A number of people had arrived and many of them were already sitting down, clutching programs for the evening's performance. Mum, who was sitting in the second row, waved to him. Dad was reading his program and didn't notice Sam. By the time Mum had nudged him, it was too late. Sam had already disappeared backstage again.

When the hall was full, the lights were dimmed and Ms Norton walked on to the stage to introduce the evening. The three actors waited in the wings and watched a string of dancers, singers, two violinists and a piano player before it was their turn to do the short scene.

Sam tried to concentrate on his lines and not think about the audience. Although he was used to crowds when he played basketball, he had never been on a stage before. Somehow, he managed to focus his thoughts. As he turned to the other two performers, both of whom were in costume, everything around him seemed to fade away. He became Ronaldo. He was the pompous circus ringmaster who was trying to outsmart the insufferably clever Waldo. Outside of the little circle of light he stood in on stage, he could hear the audience. As he lunged forward to grab Waldo, he heard them laugh. Waldo evaded him, and a few people cried out in encouragement. Then, when Sam, Miles and Jemima came together to sing, the audience was instantly quiet. Only the sounds of their voices and the piano music floated above the silence.

CHAPTER 8
Performance Preview

 Miles

"That was absolutely fabulous!" said Ms Norton, as the actors walked back into the wings. They had been waiting on the stage while the audience clapped and cheered enthusiastically. "Everyone is definitely going to want to see the play now!"

When the performances had finished, Miles walked around the front of the stage into the hall. Most people had moved out of their seats and were standing. He couldn't see where his mother had gone. As he walked through the crowd, he saw Sam greeting his parents. His mother was smiling, but his father was looking at his watch impatiently.

Without thinking, Miles stepped towards Sam.

"Hello! I'm Miles, Sam's friend," he said to Sam's parents.

Sam's mum turned. "Hello! You were absolutely terrific. What a magnificent voice you have."

"Thank you," said Miles. "Sam sounds very good, too, doesn't he?"

"He does," said Sam's mum, with just a hint of pride.

"And he's a fantastic actor, too. I'm sure you could see that," added Miles.

From behind Miles, another adult voice spoke. "We have been very fortunate that Sam was able to fill in for Miles when he broke his leg." It was Ms Norton speaking. She smiled at Sam. "We have such a talented group of actors in this play. I'm so impressed with them. Miles has been so helpful, despite his disappointment at not being able to play the lead. And as for Sam, well, he has had to juggle rehearsing for the play with playing basketball. He has been an absolute trooper."

Just then, Miles saw his parents. "I have to go," he said, excusing himself and saying goodbye. As he left, he overheard Ms Norton telling Sam's parents about how much Sam had helped and how he looked after the younger children in the cast. Miles glanced back at the adults for a second. He saw that Sam's dad was listening closely and smiling.

CHAPTER 9
Dad's Advice

 Sam

On Friday afternoon, Sam's dad was waiting for Sam at the school gate. "I organised to leave work early so I could take you to basketball practice," he said.

"You haven't been to practice for ages," said Sam.

Dad nodded. "I thought it might give us a chance to talk."

In the car, Dad continued. "I want to know how you are feeling about basketball at the moment."

"It's okay," said Sam, shrugging. "I still like playing."

"I spoke to Mr Gilmore today. He said you've been playing well and he is pleased with the effort you've been making, but if you are finding it's too much, he can rotate you with other players."

Sam thought for a moment. "I would like to keep playing if I'm good enough. I feel like I can keep up. Mr Gilmore might decide to replace me if I'm not."

"You were correct about the team, Sam," said Dad. "There are quite a few outstanding players now."

Sam laughed. "That's why we are so good, Dad. Everybody has improved. Besides, I was never the best player. You just thought I was."

It was Dad's turn to laugh. "I don't know about that! I'm still fairly certain you are the best, but I thought you were excellent on the stage, as well. Perhaps you would like to take some drama classes once all your activities have finished?"

"I would really love that, Dad," said Sam. "And maybe I could do some singing and dancing lessons, too!"

"Hmm," Dad murmured, half smiling. "We'll have to see about that."

CHAPTER 10
Showtime!

 Miles

Miles was nervous – but not because he had forgotten his lines or was worried about making a mistake on stage. He was nervous because everyone was in their costumes and the last person was having their make-up applied, but Sam hadn't arrived yet. Miles knew Sam had competed in the final of the basketball competition on the other side of town that afternoon. He thought he would be at the hall by now.

"I hope he hasn't broken his leg!" he said under his breath, as he watched the audience fill the seats in the hall.

Just then, Miles heard a loud commotion at the backstage door. Someone was hammering to come inside. Ms Norton appeared suddenly with a key and unlocked it, and Sam almost fell in as the door swung open.

"Sorry," he said. "There was so much traffic and it was difficult to –"

"It's all right!" said Ms Norton. "But you need to get your costume on quickly."

Miles didn't have time to ask Sam about the basketball game as Sam raced past him to the dressing room. Miles checked the wall clock. It was almost time for the curtain to go up. He would have to wait until after the show to find out.

As Miles hobbled onto the stage behind the curtain to take his place, he still felt nervous. Stage nerves, he realised – he was excited! He couldn't wait for everyone to be ready, for the orchestra to begin and for the curtain to go up. Everything that he and Sam and all his friends had worked for over the last two months was in place now.

The Great Waldo was about to begin!